The THREE Little PIGS

Written by Saviour Pirotta
Illustrated by Olivia Beckman

Three little pigs built themselves three little homes.

The first pig built a
house with **straw.**

The second pig built
a house with **sticks.**

The third pig
built a house
with **bricks.**

No sooner had the first pig moved into
his house than the wolf came by.

He was very hungry and he could think of
nothing more tasty than a young juicy pig.

"Little pig, little pig, let me in."

The first pig replied, "Not by the hair on my chinny chin chin."

"Then I'll **huff** and I'll **puff** and I'll **blow** your house down," roared the wolf.

So he **huffed** and he **puffed** and he **blew** the straw house down.

The little pig ran away to his sister's house made of sticks.

Soon the wolf was at the door
of that house too.

"Little pigs, little pigs, let me in."

The second pig squealed, "Not by the hair on my chinny chin chin."

"Then I'll **huff** and I'll **puff** and I'll **blow** your house down," howled the wolf.

So he **huffed** and he **puffed** and he **blew** the wooden house down.

The little pigs ran away to their
brother's house made of bricks.

The wolf soon found that house too.
He called, "Little pigs, little pigs, let me in."

The third pig replied,
"Not by the hair on my
chinny chin chin."

"Then I'll **huff** and I'll **puff** and
I'll **blow** your house down,"
shouted the wolf.

And he **huffed** and he **puffed** until he nearly **burst.**

But he could not blow the brick house down.

"Perhaps he'll go away?"
said the first pig.

The pigs cooked a pot of soup in the fireplace.

They removed the lid
and stoked up the fire.

The wolf sniggered. "I'm coming to eat you up, little pigs! One of you for breakfast, one for lunch and one for dinner!"

But he jumped right down the chimney... straight into the hot POT!

"Ouch," cried the wolf.

He hopped around the
house howling in pain.

The third pig threw
open the window and
the wolf leapt out.

The three little pigs knew he
would never bother them again.

Next Steps

Discussion and Comprehension

Ask the children the following questions and discuss their answers:
- What would've happened to the pigs if they had let the wolf in?
- What is your home built from?
- What makes this story exciting?
- What does the author mean when he said that the pigs 'stoked up the fire'?
- What do you think the wolf does after he's left the three pigs? How do you think he feels?

Looking at the Characters

Ask the children to say how each of the houses were different. For example, the first one was built of straw, the second one was built with sticks etc. Ask the children to look at the three little pigs on page 3. Ask them to compare the differences in the appearance of the pigs. Can they list the differences? If able, they could write this in three sentences:
The first little pig has got... The second little pig wears.... The third little pig has...

Huffing and Puffing Painting

Give the children a range of pots of thinly mixed paint, a large sheet of sugar paper and some plastic drinking straws. Ask them to put drops of coloured paint onto the paper and then huff and puff and blow the paint with the straw to make a pattern.